LEARN TO SHARE

FOREST FRIENDS LEARN TO SHARE
Text copyright © 1993 by Danae Dobson.
Illustrations copyright © 1993 by Cuitlahuac Morales.

Managing Editor: Laura Minchew
Project Editor: Beverly Phillips

Library of Congress Cataloging-in-Publication Data

Dobson, Danae.
   Forest friends learn to share / Danae Dobson ; illustrated by
Cuitlahuac Morales.
      p.   cm. — Forest friends series
   "Word kids!"
   Summary: In a dream, six-year-old Eric makes many new friends
among the animals of Big Green Forest and experiences the truth of
the Bible verse, "It's more blessed to give than to receive."
   ISBN 0–8499–0985–6
   [1. Forest animals—Fiction. 2. Selfishness—Fiction.
3. Sharing—Fiction. 4. Dreams—Fiction. 5. Christian life—Fiction.]
I. Morales, Cuitlahuac, 1967–   ill. II. Title.
III. Series: Dobson, Danae. Forest friends series.
PZ7.D6614Fos 1993
[E]—dc20
                                                          93–10791
                                                             CIP
                                                              AC

Printed in the United States of America
3 4 5 6 7 8 9 LBM 9 8 7 6 5 4 3 2 1

LEARN TO SHARE

DANAE DOBSON

Illustrated by Cuitlahuac Morales

WORD *Kids!*

WORD PUBLISHING

Dallas • London • Vancouver • Melbourne

Eric Martin had just turned six years old. His father had given him a new red truck for his birthday. Eric was so happy! He had wanted the truck ever since he saw it in the store window. Now it finally belonged to him!

That afternoon Eric went outside to play. He took the
new truck with him, along with his favorite stuffed dog,
Tucker. He sat down on the cool grass under a big oak tree.

Just then, he saw Tommy Merino walking toward him.
"Hi!" said Tommy. "Is that a new truck?"
"Yes," said Eric. "It was a birthday present."
"It's really cool," said Tommy. "Can I play with it, too?"

Eric didn't answer at first.

Then he said, "No! It's mine! You're always coming over and playing with my toys. Don't you have any of your own?"

Tommy looked sad as he turned to walk away.

Eric felt bad about being so mean to his friend. But after all, the truck *did* belong to him. He hadn't even played with it yet. So that's exactly what he did! But it just wasn't much fun all by himself. Pretty soon, he fell asleep under the oak tree.

Suddenly, Tucker began to bark.

"What is it, boy?" asked Eric.

He reached down to pat the toy dog on the head. But when Eric looked up, he noticed something strange.

"Hey!" he said out loud. "This isn't my front yard! Where am I?" Eric could see nothing but trees in every direction.

"I must be in some kind of forest!" he said. "Come on, Tucker. We've got to find a way out of here!"

Just then, two small rabbits hopped from behind a bush.
They looked exactly alike, except one was pink and the
other was yellow.

They stood there staring at the boy and his little dog.
Finally the yellow bunny spoke. "Who are you?"

"My name is Eric," said the boy. "This is my dog, Tucker.
Can you tell me where I am?"

"Yes," said the pink bunny. "You're in Big Green Forest. My name is Pinky, and this is my twin brother, Pookie. We live here."

"Did you say I'm in Big Green Forest?" asked Eric. "I wonder how I got here."

"Don't you know?" asked Pookie.

"No," said Eric. "I was sitting under the oak tree and . . . well, never mind. Can you tell me how to get back to the city of Cherry Creek? That's where I live."

"Sure!" said Pinky. "But first we want you to meet our friends."

"Who are they?" asked Eric.

"Come on!" said Pinky. "We'll take you to meet them!"

"Well, I guess we could stay for a little while," said Eric.

With that, he and Tucker followed the two rabbits through the forest. Before long, they reached an open meadow. Eric could see several animals playing chase in the grass.

"Hey, everybody!" shouted Pookie. "Come and meet our new friends!"

The animals ran and gathered around Eric and Tucker.
"Does your dog talk?" asked a friendly little skunk.
"No," laughed Eric, "he doesn't. He just growls and barks."
One by one, Pookie told Eric the names of his friends.
There was Oliver the Skunk, Woodrow the Beaver, and a
deer named Fawna.

"Who's that?" asked Eric, pointing to a squirrel in a nearby tree.

"Oh, that's Sidney," said Oliver. "He used to be our friend, but he's not anymore."

"Why don't you like him?" asked Eric.

"Because he's selfish," said Pinky. "Yesterday he found a pile of acorns near the riverbank. He won't share even one! He's been storing them in that old tree."

"That's right," said Fawna. "And he won't let any of us get too close. He's afraid we'll steal the acorns."

"Sidney is greedy," said Woodrow.

"And *very* selfish," added Pookie.

Eric scratched his head.

"Well, maybe I could talk to him," he said.

"It's no use," said Pookie. "Sidney would rather have his acorns than his friends."

Eric walked toward the tree. The little squirrel was busy storing acorns and didn't notice Eric at first. Suddenly his eyes opened wide.

"Stop!" he shouted. "Don't come any closer."

"Why not?" asked Eric.

"Because . . ." said the squirrel, "you're not welcome here!"

Eric smiled and folded his arms.

"Don't you think you're being selfish?" he asked.

"No!" answered Sidney. "I don't! I found these nuts, and no one can have them except me."

"What's more important?" asked Eric. "Your friends or the acorns?"

Sidney didn't answer the question. He just kept telling Eric to go away. By this time the other animals had gathered around Eric.

"Leave me alone!" shouted Sidney. "All of you! Stay away from here!"

The angry squirrel didn't see what was going on behind him. Three chipmunks had climbed up the tree to the hole where the acorns were hidden.

Suddenly Sidney heard something hit the ground. He turned quickly and looked around. The chipmunks were running across the meadow.

"Come back here!" he shouted.

But it was too late. The chipmunks were gone . . . and so were the acorns. Sidney looked at his friends. He hung his head in shame. He ran crying into the hole in the tree. In a few minutes he came out again.

"I guess I *was* being selfish. Now look what happened! I've lost everything!"

"You still have us!" said Pinky.

Sidney smiled.

"Are you sure you still want to be friends with me?"

All the animals shouted and cheered. They were glad that Sidney was back to his old self again.

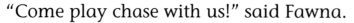

"Come play chase with us!" said Fawna.

"All right," said the squirrel. "That sounds like a lot more fun than fighting over acorns."

Eric and the animals had a wonderful time playing chase games. Even Sidney was enjoying the fun.

Finally, it was time for Eric to go home. Pookie and Pinky offered to help him find his way back. As they set off through the woods, the other animals waved good-bye. Eric promised to return someday for another visit.
Before long, the rabbits had taken their two new friends to the entrance of Big Green Forest.

"I can see my house from here," said Eric. "Thanks for helping me find my way home."

The two bunnies stood waving as Eric and Tucker headed down the hill.

"Wasn't that fun?" asked Eric, looking down at the little dog.

Tucker barked and wagged his tail.

"You know, I learned a lesson about selfishness, too," said Eric. "The Bible verse my Sunday school teacher quotes is true: 'It's more blessed to give than to receive.' Tucker, I'm going to really try to never be greedy or selfish again."

Just then, Eric opened his eyes. He yawned sleepily and looked around. Why, he was still under the oak tree. There by his side was Tucker and his new red truck, just where he had left them.

"It was only a dream," Eric said to himself. "The rabbit twins, Sidney, Big Green Forest . . . it was all a dream!"

Eric stood up and stretched. In the distance he could see Tommy Merino. Tommy was bouncing a basketball in front of his garage door.

Without waiting another minute, Eric picked up Tucker and his new toy. Then he ran over to Tommy's house.

"I'm sorry for being so mean and selfish earlier today," said Eric. "I brought my new truck over—let's play with it together."

"All right," said Tommy. "I'll go get some of my trucks to play with, too.

Eric sat down on the porch to wait for his friend. He thought about Big Green Forest and the animals that were in his dream. He was glad they helped him learn to share with his friends.